THE BEWILDERED

HAYLEY MEDINA

Printed in the United States of America

KMP Entertainment (Publishing Division)

www.kmpentertainment.org

ISBN: 979-8-9866628-7-9

CHAPTER 1

North For the Summer

School's out. The smell of a nice summer breeze is in the air. The scorching sun hits my skin. That's my definition of paradise. So why do I have to spend my summer in Forks, an icy cold place where I don't think they know what the sun is!

Mom exclaimed anxiously "Sara, are you done packing yet? We need to leave soon if you want to catch the plane!"

"I'm all done with packing. Can you ask dad to help me with the luggage," I queried. Then for good measure I added "I guess this is the last time I'll get to wear shorts this summer."

My mom thought it would be nice to spend time with my cousins this summer. I haven't seen them in 2 years, so I was excited to see them again. And don't get me wrong, I love hanging out with them. It's just so cold where they moved. I personally love the heat and don't prefer getting frostbite.

"Mom why do I have to go all the way to Forks. Why can't they just come down here where there's ice cream and we can swim in nice cold pools."

"It won't kill you to be in the cold for three weeks. Try to enjoy it. I mean you could go sledding there, or a snowball fight which you can't do here because we never get snow, especially in summer."

"If the cold is so amazing, then why aren't you coming with me."

"Because, Sara, wouldn't it be nice to just have some alone time with your cousins."

Yeah right, she's just making up excuses because she doesn't want to freeze in the cold, I think to myself.

"Now don't forget to cover up. It gets very cold."

"I know, Mom. Don't worry. I love you

I'll see you later."

"Don't forget to call me every night."

"Don't worry, I won't. Goodbye, Mom."

And just like that I was on a plane

heading over to my aunt's house. I've always

been afraid of heights so, planes and I don't

mix well. No one would catch me dead sitting

at a window seat I made sure I was smack

dab in the middle of the plane. I was

terrified! This was the first time I was on a

plane without my mom here comforting me.
I was there for what felt like years.

When I got to the airport it was almost
empty. I went outside to meet up with my
aunt. The sun had pretty much already set
outside. The sky looked pretty with a red tint
and light pink cotton candy clouds. I looked
around and saw my Aunt Jessica welcoming
me with a warm smile.

She was standing there shivering. She had
a huge fluffy coat, a scarf, mittens, ear muffs
the whole package and more. As I was

walking toward her, she wrapped her coat tighter around her to shield herself from the cold. I guess she doesn't like the cold either.

She has captivating, icy blue eyes and blonde hair. I've always been told that my aunt and I look more like mother and daughter than my actual mom and I do. I got in the car and we started to head to her place.

They had moved into the new house that's been under construction for a while, so I was excited to see it. I'm pretty sure that Aunt Jessica helped design most of the house. I think they decided to build it from the ground up. I couldn't wait to see the product of her hard work.

"So, I know you must not be too excited about spending your entire summer here. I know how much you hate the cold," Aunt Jessica whispered.

"It's fine I don't mind; I can deal with it. I'm excited to see my cousins more than anything. I can't wait."

"Elisabeth and Abby were so excited. They've been counting down the days until you would be here. They were so upset when they couldn't come with me to come pick you up, but that's what they get for not doing their chores. We're about twenty seven minutes away from the house," Aunt Jessica told me.

Ugh. They lived so far away from town.

While she was driving, I noticed when I looked to my left or my right all I could see were trees surrounding us. There were very few lights to brighten the road and there weren't any other cars around. The lights were only meant for the road so everything around it was dark.

I could see the outline of the trees only because the moonlight gave them a subtle glow, but I couldn't see the top of the trees because of how tall they were.

We had been driving for a while and went so far that I couldn't even see the town lights anymore. I was nodding off in the car because I was so tired from the flight. I was trying so hard to keep my eyes open, but my eyelids felt too heavy. Eventually I gave in and fell asleep" When my aunt woke me up, I was awe struck, we had turned down their street.

I took a glance and there were only 4 to 5 houses around and the neighbors were so far spaced from each other. We got closer to my aunt's home, and it looked like her house was glowing because all the lights were on since it was late at night. It was huge and painted a comforting cream color.

I thought the cream shade complemented the snow that was on the roof and surrounding the house. It had 2 stories I'm pretty sure it would have taken up a lot more room if it wasn't for the trees. There were a lot of windows, and the garage was huge. I couldn't wait to see the backyard.

As we pulled into the driveway, I saw Elisabeth and Abby sprinting toward the car. Elisabeth was 15, and 3 years older than Abby. They didn't really look like sisters. Elisabeth had long beautiful blonde hair with light blue eyes. She has always been so stylish! She was currently wearing a cute white crop top and ripped jeans. I guess she liked the cold, but just looking at her was enough to make me shiver.

She looked like a younger version of my aunt and by default looked more like my sister. Abby had short dark brown hair with brown eyes, she had a black long-sleeved shirt on with high-waisted jeans. She looked like her father's "mini-me".

As they brought me inside, I met the most charming puppy I have ever seen. Her name was Sapphire. She was a cute husky with a white coat and one brown eye and one blue eye, and she had a red collar.

The inside of their house looked so pretty and clean. The floors were shining, everything looked nice and I was scared to touch it because I didn't want anything to get dirty.

"So how do you like our new place?" Elisabeth asked.

"Hey, you want to come check out my room, it's the coolest place in the house. I spent so much time making sure it looked perfect," Abby said with excitement in her voice.

She sounded so happy and like she really wanted to show me, but I was running low on energy. I tried to figure out a way to try and let her down. I enjoy spending time with her, but she just has so much energy it's like she never runs out.

"It's always a huge mess in your room. Last time I saw it I couldn't see the floor," Elisabeth whined.

"I cleaned so it doesn't look messy anymore. Follow me it's up the stairs you're going to love it." Abby said with a smile

"Let Sara breath. She's had a long flight and she probably just wants to relax," Aunt Jessica directed.

There was no way I could handle going upstairs and having to act like I'm fascinated with everything she wants to show me.

"Sorry guys I'm pretty tired. Would you mind if we just watched TV for a little bit? I'm jet lagged."

"Yea sure I'd be up for that want to watch a movie" Elisabeth.

"But I want to show Sara my room there still so much time. We could make cookies, tell scary stories, play hide and go seek," Abby excitedly chimed in.

"Sara wants to relax so leave her alone," said Elisabeth

"Elisabeth don't be rude to your sister. Try to watch a movie you would all like. And Abby, I already said to let Sara relax. It's almost midnight, there's no time to make cookies, you have the entire summer to do all that, so for tonight let Sara get all her energy back. Tomorrow we can plan something to do," Aunt Jessica declared.

I was so tired I could barely talk I thought I was going to pass out.

"Hey, I'm just thinking I'm going to head to bed. I don't think I'd be able to finish the movie with you guys."

"Ok that's fine sweetie your room is on the 2nd floor, third door on the right I can show you if you want." Aunt Jessica offered. "No, its fine I can find it on my own. Thank you for having me over I can't wait to have fun with you guys this summer goodnight."

CHAPTER 2

The Boy First Appeared

When I woke up I was so tired I couldn't even remember where I was.

It seemed like it was around eight in the morning. I was too exhausted to get up and check the time. The only reason I woke up was because of the smell of eggs and bacon filling my room. I was so hungry. All I had on the airplane was peanuts and water, not exactly a five-star, three course meal. I finally got the strength to get up and drag myself down the stairs.

When I got to the kitchen, I was so happy I saw breakfast on the dining room table. It felt like I hadn't eaten in years. I was practically drooling on the floor. The only person I saw was Aunt Jessica cooking food over the stove. I think I was the first one to wake up.

"Good morning, Sara how did you

sleep?" Aunt Jessica queried.

"I slept really well. As soon as I hit the mattress, I fell asleep, and I slept like a log."

"That's good I'm glad you slept well. You can go ahead and dig in. No one is awake yet. I hope it's ok I forgot to ask you what you wanted for breakfast so I decided that you can never go wrong with the classics," Aunt Jessica teased.

I was so hungry that it wouldn't matter if she just got toasted bread and put butter on it, I would have still thought it would taste like heaven to eat.

"It looks great, Aunt Jessica! Thank you so much. I'll go ahead and eat."

While I was stuffing my face full of eggs, I heard footsteps coming down the stairs. Abby, Elisabeth, and Uncle Jacob had all awakened at the same time. Even Sapphire was trotting behind Elisabeth. It looked like they had all planned to come down at the same time.

They even rubbed their eyes at the same time as if all their Bluetooth's had synced up with each other. We all decided to go into town to watch a movie around 3 o'clock. I didn't really want to go anywhere because that would mean I would have to go outside. I wanted to stay inside where I knew the warmth wouldn't flee me.

After finishing breakfast my aunt Jessica said she wanted to talk to me. I just assumed it would be some house rules or I don't know maybe she'd tell me about curfew or something. She would not have to worry about that with me, though, because there's no way I would leave the house unless we all had plans to do something.

As we moved to the living room and got to the couch, I sat down. She seemed very serious. It kind of shocked me. I had never seen that sort of face on my aunt before. It looked like she was confused or not sure how to tell me something.

"So, Sara, this isn't a story to try and scare you with, but if you are going to be staying with us these next few weeks there is something you need to know." Aunt Jessica said in a hushed voice.

I didn't know what to expect when she said that. She brought it up like it was a life-or-death sort of situation it was kind of freaking me out.

"I can say this from experience that this isn't just a story. As you can very well see, we are surrounded by the woods. When we first moved into the house, it wasn't finished being built yet. All that was left, though, was the pool in the backyard.

The construction workers said they kept

seeing and hearing things in the forest out back. At first, I just thought that maybe they were working too hard or just didn't get enough sleep, but the complaints about wild animals or strange figures kept showing up. Quite a few men didn't want to keep working here because of some of the stuff they had heard or thought they might have seen. We finally decided to call the police hoping it would put their worried minds at ease. After all, if it was a person they would be trespassing since this is private property. The police said they didn't see anyone while looking around but that they did see some shoeprints and a lot of broken branches.

Your uncle and I were shocked to find that out. We felt bad for doubting the workers and pushing their worries aside. We had no clue how to proceed from there. The police said the shoeprints couldn't be any bigger than a child's shoeprints. We thought that maybe if it was a child, they needed help. The police said that there weren't any missing children's cases anywhere in this location.

It took thirty minutes just to get to town

from here. The police decided to put together a search party hoping to find the child. They went out in the morning. There were fifteen people helping including both me and your uncle Jacob. We started the search at nine that morning, and we decided to split up into groups of two hoping to divide and conquer. Uncle Jacob and I were looking near where the shoeprints were, but we didn't find anyone. We kept looking until seven pm. That's when I heard something run behind me. I was with your uncle. He heard it, too, and we called out, hoping it was the child.

But no one answered and we saw the child running across from us about eight yards away. This time we saw the child was a little boy no older than thirteen years old, with dark brown hair, a blue navy shirt and blue jeans. I called out saying that I just wanted to help him and that I wasn't going to hurt him. He just stood there. He didn't move or make any noise.

I walked to where he was. I explained that I was there to help him, but when I got close, he ran. I sprinted closely behind him, and Uncle Jacob went chasing after me. I went to where I saw him run, but he was gone. Like he had disappeared into thin air. Uncle Jacob was just as shocked as I was.

I saw one of the other search parties just a few feet away from us. We went and asked them if they had seen the boy. And they said that they had followed him here. We explained that the same thing happened to us.

All of us were confused because he had been in both places at once. We started to look for him together but ended up nowhere. Eventually we had to go back and regroup with the others we had run out of time it was already dark outside.

We didn't want to run into any wild animals. The police didn't know what to do either. They said that we had already reached out to help so just leave it alone. We tried again in the morning but didn't get anywhere, we couldn't find him. Eventually the police said that we were getting nowhere and that maybe we had just seen a deer or animal that looked like a boy. But I knew what I saw, and it was no animal.

I felt bad for leaving the boy out there. It felt like I was giving up on him. I started to think about it and thought that maybe it was a ghost or a figment of my imagination, but Uncle Jacob saw him, too, which only left the option of him being a ghost.

We asked our neighbors if they had seen a boy around their property, but they said that they didn't see anything weird or suspicious like that. I started to wonder if maybe we had disturbed him or maybe he just wanted to be left alone.

What I'm trying to say is we don't know what's out there or who but let's not find out anytime soon. It didn't seem like he had any bad intentions, but I still don't trust it. So please don't go into the forest in the backyard. It isn't safe and I don't want you getting lost or something happening to you." Aunt Jessica shared.

I don't know what I expected to hear when I sat down but it sure wasn't that I didn't know how to react. Ever since I was a kid, I've always been an adrenaline junkie. I love ghost stories, legends, tests of courage, all that kind of stuff. When I heard my aunt telling the story, I got chills down my spine.

I couldn't help but let my curiosity get to me. I really wanted to know what was out there. I love hearing the stories but experiencing them is so cool. I understood that my aunt just wanted to protect me, but I really wanted to go to the forest to find out for myself. But sadly, I wasn't going to do that, I didn't want to go against my aunt's wishes. The last thing I would want is to worry her.

"Don't worry I understand, I won't go in the forest. Plus, it's too cold to try and go on an adventure."

I joked around trying to ease her mind...

Memories In the Snow

had a lot of fun with my family. Time flew by! I couldn't believe it had already been a week since I got here. I've had so much fun despite how, at first, I thought I wouldn't be able to enjoy myself because of the cold.   Surprisingly it didn't hold me back much.

Abby, Elizabeth, and I got to do many things in a short period of time. We built forts, and even though it's freezing here, they built a pool in the back yard. It was so warm! The pool was more or less connected to the house. There were windows bult in with the structure which meant we had a clear view of the woods out back. Every single time I glanced over to the woods I would be so tempted to just run out and explore, but I stayed away, trying to avoid it because I was too tempted.

I couldn't help but wonder who was out

there. I wanted to find out their story and find out who they were and what life they lived. I had so many questions that I wanted answered but didn't have anyone to answer them. I tried to forget about it but the more I tried to forget the more I started thinking about it. Sometimes, at night, I would feel someone staring at me from beyond the living room windows. I decided it was my imagination and brushed it off.

One night, Aunt Jessica and Uncle Jacob needed to go run errands, so it was just me, Abby, and Elisabeth in the house. I think they said they would be back around eight that evening.

I wanted to do something. I was sick of being inside and watching movies. I wanted to go outside even though I wanted to stay warm. It looked so beautiful out there the snow made everything sparkle. I wanted to take in all the scenery and appreciate everything around me. I decided to go and ask Abby and Elisabeth if they wanted to come with me outside.

They both said that it would be fun to go

outside and play in the snow. We all got our coats on and went outside. While we started to head out to the backyard, I saw how excited their dog, Sapphire, was, and I just couldn't leave her behind. Her face was saying "let's all play together," so I decided to let her come outside with us.

I started to think maybe the cold isn't all bad. As soon as I got outside, I remembered why I didn't like the cold and regretted even thinking about coming out here. As I was about to suggest we should go back inside I felt something hit my back. I turned around and it was Abby with snowballs in her hand.

I didn't even get the chance to comprehend what was going on before

Abby yelled "Snowball Fight!"

Elisabeth took cover behind the trampoline, and I went to go behind the outside of the pool house. I started to gather snow. That way I could make some snowballs. Before I could even make my second snowball, though, out of the corner of my eye, I saw Elisabeth about to throw a snowball at me.

Before she could do that, I grabbed the first snowball I made and threw it right in her face. She was dumbfounded. Even Sapphire didn't know how to react. She was so confused with all the chaos.

I wanted to laugh so hard because of how shocked she looked, but I didn't have any time to laugh because approaching to my left was Abby. She decided to take advantage of this situation and thought she caught me off guard, but I grabbed Elisabeth and used her as a shield.

After the snowball hit Elisabeth, we all froze and couldn't help but burst into laughter. We all decided to have a fresh start. We had 20 seconds to make snowballs then after the time was up it was a free for all. It was so much fun playing in the snow.

Even though I had gloves on I started to lose feeling in my fingers, but I didn't even pay any attention to it because if I let my guard down even for a little bit, I knew I would get hit with a snowball. Time had flown by so quickly it was already 7:35 pm I couldn't feel my face. And it was getting dark outside.

We all decided to take a break and head inside for a little bit to get warmed up and my get something to eat. I felt like we were forgetting something but couldn't remember. When we went inside, I decided to look outside. I saw something white jump over the backyard fence and run into the forest. It was sapphire!

We completely forgot to take her inside with us. I yelled, getting Abby and Elisabeth's attention.

"Sapphire went into the forest!"

We all ran outside and didn't see her anywhere. Abby started to panic

"What are we going to do? It's almost eight! Mom's going to get so mad."

"Stop freaking out! It'll be fine. We just need to go into the forest and get her back home. She couldn't have gone that far," Elisabeth sighed.

"But you know Mom said we shouldn't

because of the ghost. And plus, it's already dark out. There could be wild animals and we could get lost," Abby whined.

"Yes, but if we just leave her out there, she could get eaten by those wild animals you're scared of. I think we should just find her, get her out of the forest and no one will know. It'll be like it never happened and we won't get in trouble. What do you think Sara,?" Elisabeth asked me.

I didn't know how to answer. I wanted to get sapphire out of the forest as soon as possible and still not go against my aunts wishes but they were still at least twenty minutes.

"Ok I have a plan. Elisabeth and I will go into the forest and try to find Sapphire. Abby, you will stay here and call Aunt Jessica and tell her what's happening.

Elisabeth and I got our coats on. We grabbed our phones so that we would have flashlights and went outside while Abby got the phone and called Aunt Jessica. I can't deny that there was a little part of me happy, but I also felt bad doing the exact thing my aunt told me not to do. Not to mention I didn't want anything bad happening to Sapphire.

I didn't want to be happy because of the situation so I was more worried that anything. While I opened the gate to go into the forest, I felt this huge pit in my stomach. I felt like I was going to throw up because of how nervous I was. I took a deep breath trying to calm myself down thinking thoughts like 'Sapphire's going to be ok,' and 'there's nothing to worry about.' Though for some reason my brain starts to think about the worst-case scenarios when I'm in bad situations. Elisabeth thought that we should split up. I thought we should stick together.

Elisabeth said, "We can cover more ground and find sapphire fast if we split up."

I couldn't disagree with that and couldn't find any reason not to split up, we don't have to be alone if we get lost. But I thought that was a stupid reason to try and stick together so we split up. Before we left to go into the forest, I told Elisabeth to come back no matter what in less than fifteen minutes.

We both put a timer on our phone and agreed on that. I didn't know what to expect once we started to leave our haven and started to go into this place, we knew almost nothing about. My heart was dropped to my stomach, and I felt this huge knot in my throat.

Maybe I was curious when I heard the story but now, I knew that I didn't want to go into that forest even if my aunt told me not to. We both split up and began our search.

Best case scenario, we find the dog and get

out of here before my uncle and aunt come

home. Worst case scenario, we both get lost

and can't find the dog and end up in the

same search rescue we went on thinking we

could do with ease.

CHAPTER 4

The Boy In the Woods

The moment I stepped foot into the forest, I became hypersensitive. I heard all the birds, all the branches. All of them. I could even hear my own breathing. I was using my flashlight to help avoid branches because I wanted to be able to hear my surroundings more. It was so dark outside.

I had barely got into the forest and moved a few feet away and I could barely see the lights from the house. I tried to focus on finding sapphire. I didn't know what to do besides search. I was hoping she would respond if I said her name, but I didn't know if she'd come to me.

There was no point in not trying. I tried yelling for her, but I heard nothing. I stopped calling her name so loud in fear that something else would find me. I just kept looking instead of yelling.

The atmosphere changed dramatically, it started to feel so heavy. I felt off I had chills coming down my spine. I started to feel so scared but had no reason to. I could feel my unease turning into anxiety. Then I heard branches break.

As I turned to find out what it was something had emerged from the darkness. I was terrified and my heart started to race. My mind couldn't comprehend what my eyes were seeing. It was the boy there staring at me. I kept thinking it was a dream. I mean, it had to be, right? There's no way this could be real. He looked so pale, almost identical to a doll.

Internally, I couldn't calm down. He was right in front of me! There was no denying it my aunt wasn't making stuff up. I had to believe he was real.

I shined my light at him, hoping it would scare him off, but when I did, he didn't even flinch. He started to walk toward me. I started to panic.

With my adrenaline rushing through my veins, I couldn't think clearly. All I could think of is "Run" and "I don't want to die!" Those thoughts kept rushing through my head. I didn't know what to do. I wanted to run but my body wouldn't move.

He started to get closer, so I started running. Finally, after what felt like a century, my legs started to move, and I ran as fast as I could. I thought I had put some distance between us, but when I got enough courage to look behind me, he was close. He was slowly but surely catching up with me. Or maybe I was just slowing down? A new thought entered my head. What if I just stopped running? What would happen?

A new possibility opened up. I started to calm down and question things. Why is he chasing me? What did I do wrong? Why was I scared I was going to get killed it's not like he has a knife. Why did I start running? Was it just because I was feeling scared? Why does he scare me? I stopped running. I was going to have to stop anyway. My lungs hurt so much, and my legs felt numb. I was panting so much it hurt to breath because of the icy cold air. It was quiet . . . too quiet.

I turned around to look at him. I looked with fear expecting him to be there. But there was no one there. He had disappeared. I could have sworn he was right behind me, but I didn't see him. The adrenaline was rushing through me, so I hadn't noticed where I was running to. I just thought in the moment that I needed to get away.

I didn't notice I was in the middle of nowhere. I couldn't see the house at all. Just as I was starting to worry again, I heard this loud noise. It scared me half to death.

It was my alarm going off on my phone. I almost had a heart attack. I wanted to get back to the house, but I had no clue where I was. All I could see was the trees. Then I saw a figure in the shadows.

I was completely sure that it was the boy. I walked toward it, hoping it would be the same thing I was running from. Now that I was a little calmer, I had questions that I wanted answers to.

Why did you chase after me? And what happened to you? What kind of life did you live? I felt like I needed the answer. To my surprise, he ran away as soon as I walked toward him. I didn't want to be alone, and I wanted to find out who he was. Before I knew it, I was chasing him. He always stayed in my sight, but I never got close enough to ask him anything.

I chased him for quite some time, I was so tired. Then suddenly, he stopped. I looked up and I was at my cousin's house.

While I was looking at the house, he disappeared again.

I never found any answers to my questions. Instead, I had a bunch of new questions. Was he just trying to help me get back? Did he know I was lost? Was he not trying to scare me but trying to help me this entire time? Why did he approach me in the first place I wasn't lost then?

My head felt heavy with all these questions rushing in at the same time like a flood. And I was still so tired from running I just wanted to sleep. I went into the house.

Everyone was relieved I was there.

Aunt Jessica and Uncle Jacob were

home. I looked past them and saw Elisabeth

with Sapphire. I was so happy she found her.

Before I walked into the house, they were

about to call the police to help find me. They

were scared that I might have gotten lost or

worse.

After things calmed down of course me

and Elisabeth got scolded. Not only for

leaving Sapphire outside, but also going into

the forest and splitting up and not sticking together. There was a huge voice in my head wanting to tell Elisabeth 'I told you so,' but it didn't seem like the right time. We had more responsibility since we are the older ones, which also meant we took most of the heat for this entire situation.

Abby didn't really get a lecture like us because all she did was stay at the house and called Aunt Jessica. After Aunt Jessica finished telling us all the bad things that could've happened, she hugged both of us and whispered under her breath that she was so happy we were safe.

I talked to Aunt Jessica and told her what happened in the forest. She started thinking about it. Maybe when she was in the forest, he thought she was lost too and that's why he led her to the other group.

I was so tired I had enough adventure for the summer. Time flew by and just like that it was already time for me to start heading back home. I was sad having to leave already, I feel like there wasn't enough time. I made

good memories with them, and I'll cherish
them forever.

I still wonder what happened in that
forest to this day, but I guess I'll never find
out. I have no clue if it's a good memory or a
bad one. I was terrified, but curious.

So that's my story of what happened that
night. I don't know if he was a figure of my
imagination, or if he was a real boy that was
maybe lost to. He also could've been a ghost.
All I know is that I'm safe and got back home
in one piece, that's a good enough ending for

me. Who knows, maybe it would be good to

go visit them again next year for summer.
69